PETS *FROM* SPACE

ROCKET RIDE

Collect all the PETS FROM SPACE *books*

☐ Splash Landing
☐ Cosmic Claws
☐ Monkey Madness
☑ Rocket Ride

Also by Jan Burchett and Sara Vogler

SAM SILVER: UNDERCOVER PIRATE

Skeleton Island
The Ghost Ship
Kidnapped
The Deadly Trap
Dragon Fire
The Double-cross
The Great Rescue
The Treasure Map
The Sea Monster
Dead Man's Hand

PETS FROM SPACE

ROCKET RIDE

Jan Burchett and Sara Vogler

Illustrated by Alex Paterson

Orion
Children's Books

First published in Great Britain in 2015
by Orion Children's Books
an imprint of the Hachette Children's Group
and published by Hodder and Stoughton Limited
Orion House
5 Upper St Martin's Lane
London WC2H 9EA
An Hachette UK company

1 3 5 7 9 10 8 6 4 2

A catalogue record for this book is available from the British Library.

ISBN 978 1 4440 1186 9

Printed in Great Britain by Clays Ltd, St Ives plc

www.orionbooks.co.uk

For Harry Borg

J.B. & S.V.

For Ralph

A.P.

CONTENTS

Blast Off

Tom Bright was riding along the road on his scooter.

He was heading for Zack's house.

They were going to the town museum to do a science project for school, all about the planets.

They had arranged to meet their friend Daisy there.

Tom's dog Fizz was sitting on the back of the scooter, waving his trumpet nose in excitement.

Dogs don't usually have trumpet noses.

And they're not usually purple with yellow spots.

Fizz was a very unusual dog.

In fact he wasn't a dog at all.

He was really a Satnik from the planet Saturn. He was just pretending to be a dog – a very rare satapoodle.

And he wasn't the only Satnik. There were others, all pretending to be Earth pets. Their spaceship had splash-landed in Tom's pond. They were on a secret mission to investigate Earth.

Tom, Zack and Daisy knew they
mustn't tell anyone about their alien
friends. Grown-ups could be very silly
about aliens.

Tom screeched to a halt at Zack's gate.
Zack came running down the path and
jumped on behind Fizz.

"Museum here we come!" he yelled.

Two antennae popped out of Zack's backpack.

It was Zack's cat, Zingle.

Zingle wasn't really a cat.

Cats don't usually have antennae.

And they're not usually blue.

Zingle was a Satnik too. She was just pretending to be a cat – a very rare blue mop-haired cat.

"You're going much too slowly," she squeaked.

"My scooter doesn't go very fast with all of us on board," said Tom.

"Is it electric?" squeaked Zingle.

"Yes," said Tom. "It's got a battery."

"Silly Earthling," squeaked Zingle. "Why didn't you say? I'll get out my Satpad and use my super Satpower."

Ping!

A silver cube shot out of her fur, transformed itself into a tiny computer and landed on her paw.

Zingle tapped the keys. "Hold tight!" she squeaked.

Whizz! Bang! Crackle!

A sparkling beam of light shot out of her Satpad and hit the scooter.

The scooter leapt forwards and shot through the town.

It skidded between the lamp posts.

It screeched round the corners.

It scattered the people on the pavement.

"Cosmic!" yelled Tom. "Museum coming up!"

"Help!" shouted Zack in alarm. "We're going too fast!"

Crash!

They hit the museum door and fell in a heap.

Daisy ran up to them.

"What happened?" she asked. "You were going at a million miles an hour!"

Zingle proudly waved her Satpad. "I did that."

Tom and Zack scrambled to their feet.

"You should be more careful!" said a squawky voice.

A parrot with whiskers and a duck's bill flew out of Daisy's backpack, got his wings in a tangle and landed on his head.

"I meant to do that!" he squawked.
"I was investigating the pavement."

Gronk was Daisy's parrot.

Parrots don't usually have duckbills.

And they don't usually have whiskers.

Gronk was another Satnik. He was just
pretending to be a parrot – a very rare
duck-billed parrotpuss.

"Let's get inside," squeaked Zingle.
"I want to see the cows."

"There aren't any cows in the museum,"
said Daisy.

"Of course there are," said Gronk. "It's
a mooseum, after all. It'll be full of cows
going moo. I'll show you."

He twiddled his whiskers with his wing.

Ping!

A Satpad flew out of his feathers.

8

He caught it with his foot and tapped
the keys with his duck bill. An image
shimmered in the air.

"Your Satpads are getting their animal facts mixed up again," said Zack.

"I think the sprungles are still flobbered," said Gronk.

"Weren't you going to mend them yesterday, Fizz?" asked Daisy.

"Zoops!" said Fizz. "I forgot. I was too busy investigating the fish tank."

"Don't cows live in mooseums then?" Zingle looked puzzled.

"No," said Tom. "They live on farms."

"This is a space museum," said Zack. "It's full of exhibits about space!"

Fizz scratched his head. "We know about space already," he said.

"But Earthlings don't," squeaked Zingle. "Let's find out what funny ideas they've got."

"You've got to hide in our backpacks first," said Daisy.

"We don't need to hide!" squawked Gronk. "Everyone thinks we're Earth pets."

"Earth pets aren't allowed in museums," explained Tom.

"You'll have to stay in the backpacks until we're inside," said Daisy.

Fizz, Zingle and Gronk dived into their hiding places. Tom, Zack and Daisy hurried into the museum.

The man at the ticket desk frowned at their bulging backpacks. "You can't take those in," he said.

"But all our books are in them," said Daisy quickly.

"You can take your books," said the ticket man firmly, "but the backpacks stay here. It's the rules."

Tom, Zack and Daisy went into a huddle.

"What are we going to do?" whispered Zack.

"We could say the Satniks are new alien models," Tom whispered back. "And we're delivering them."

"They're too wriggly for models!" answered Zack.

"We could tie them on our heads and pretend they're hats," suggested Tom.

"They're too noisy for hats," said Daisy.

"I've got it!" declared Tom. "We could shout 'Look out for the fierce tiger!' and while he's looking out, the Satniks could sneak in."

"That won't work either," said Daisy. "You don't get many fierce tigers in a space museum. We'll have to do what he says."

Tom, Zack and Daisy gave their bags to the ticket man.

"Sorry, Satniks," whispered Tom.

"We won't be long," whispered Zack.

"Hurry up!" came Zingle's squeaky voice.

"Did that backpack say something?" asked the ticket man suspiciously.

"Backpacks can't talk!" said Tom.

That was true – well, apart from the one that had said "Pick me up!" to him once in a shop.

☆   ☆   ☆

Tom, Zack and Daisy wandered through some rooms with lots of space rocks on shelves.

"This museum's boring without the Satniks," said Tom.

"I can't see anything interesting for a project about the planets," said Zack.

At that moment they heard a terrible noise. It sounded like a road drill. It was coming from a room with a sign that said *Our Solar System*.

"I didn't know space was so loud," said Tom.

They stuffed their fingers in their ears and ran to the door to have a look.

In the middle of the room stood a big model planet on a stand. It had colourful rings round its middle.

"That's Saturn!" exclaimed Daisy.

"I wish the Satniks could see it," said Tom.

The floor was covered in scissors and glue and cardboard. Saturn was covered in peculiar-looking cardboard creatures. The terrible noise was even louder.

Tom, Zack and Daisy crept around the model.

Fizz, Zingle and Gronk were there, covered in glue and bits of cardboard.

"Hello," said Gronk, poking his Satpad with his bill. The terrible noise stopped. "It's a good thing we escaped from your backpacks. This model of our planet was all wrong."

"It didn't have any flinglefroobs or fratterflops on it!" squeaked Zingle. "So I've made some."

"And I was using my super Satpower," said Gronk. "It was playing the lovely song of the four-legged glugboobler."

"And I'm sticking some minglemangles on," called Fizz.

"It's cosmic!" cried Tom.

"It is *not* cosmic," said Daisy. "We could get told off for this mess."

"Let's get out of here," said Zack, "before the ticket man comes."

"We can't go yet," squeaked Zingle. "We haven't put that right." She pointed to a list on the wall.

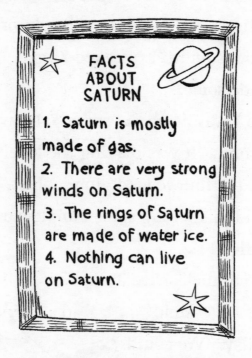

FACTS ABOUT SATURN

1. Saturn is mostly made of gas.
2. There are very strong winds on Saturn.
3. The rings of Saturn are made of water ice.
4. Nothing can live on Saturn.

"Fizz has made a much better list," said Gronk. "Show them, Fizz."

"Fizz is good at lists," squeaked Zingle. Fizz tapped some keys on his Satpad and a list wobbled in the air.

Fizz's important list of facts about Saturn by Fizz

1. Saturn is mostly made of squiqilastic which is soft and spongy.
2. There are warm breezes on Saturn.
3. The rings of Saturn are very slippery which means they're good for sliding races.
4. There is lots of life on Saturn.
5. There are Satniks for a start.
6. And flinglefroobs, fratterflops, glugbooblers, knock-kneed satcrows, klapsquabblers, lesser spotted dringpeckers, dancing satcrubs, twittering twitwumbles, warbling wickertops, minglemangles...

"Those facts on the wall need to be put right," said Gronk, picking up a crayon in his bill. "Without delay!"

"That's not a good idea," warned Daisy.

But it was too late.

19

Zingle hopped onto Fizz's head.

Gronk hopped onto Zingle's head.

He began to scrawl in big wobbly writing on the wall.

"What's going on in here?" came a loud voice and Tom turned to see the ticket man storming in.

The Satniks hid.

"Have you been messing with the display?" asked the ticket man crossly.

"Not us," said Tom. "It was like that when we came in."

"Well someone has," grumbled the ticket man. "It's all wrong now. Saturn doesn't look like that." He gave one of the cardboard creatures a poke. "What's this?"

"It's a fratterflop, silly Earthling," squeaked Zingle.

"What?" gasped the man.

"It's a fratterflop," said Daisy in a squeaky voice. "They're a new form of life."

"They've just found them on Saturn," said Zack.

"It was on telly last night," added Tom.

"Was it?" asked the man.

Ring! Ring!

Somewhere a telephone was ringing. The ticket man ran off to answer it.

"That was lucky," said Zack.

"*That* was my super Satpower," said Gronk proudly. "I frightened him away with the cry of the fierce zonglebeast."

"The fierce zonglebeast sounds just like an Earth phone," Daisy told him. "He ran off to answer it."

"Are you sure?" asked Gronk.

"Positive," said Daisy.

"I knew that," said Gronk.

"Come on," said Tom. "We still need to find something for our school project."

In the next room stood a line of robots.

Their eyes snapped open as the friends entered.

"He-llo!" said the robots.

"Hello funny Earthlings!" squeaked Zingle. "My name's Zingle. Who are you?"

"Good-bye," said the robots.

Their eyes snapped shut.

"Silly Earthlings," squeaked Zingle.

"They're not Earthlings," said Tom. "They're robots."

"They don't do much," said Fizz.

"The robots on Saturn are much better," said Gronk.

"These robots need help!" squeaked Zingle.

"No they don't!" cried Zack.

But it was too late.

Ping!

Zingle's Satpad shot out from her fur.
She tapped the keys.

Whizz! Bang! Crackle!

A sparkling beam of light shot across
the room and hit the robots.

The robots turned cartwheels.

They played football with the
wastepaper bin.

They walked upside-down on the ceiling.

"Cosmic!" yelled Tom.

"Interesting," squeaked Zingle. "They
don't do that on Saturn."

But the robots began to rattle and shake. Steam shot from their ears and their eyes pinged out on stalks.

"Very interesting," squeaked Zingle. "They don't do that on Saturn either."

The robots' arms whirled round.

Bang!

Their heads flew off.

Clunk!

The robots fell in a heap – on top of Zingle.

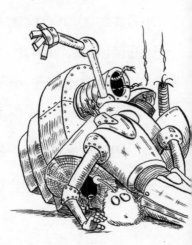

"Even more interesting," she squeaked. "They definitely don't do that on Saturn."

"What's going on in here?" came a cross voice.

The ticket man ran into the room.

Fizz and Gronk jumped into the wastepaper bin.

"Have you been messing with the robots?" demanded the ticket man.

"No," said Tom.

"Well someone has," said the ticket man, looking around suspiciously.

He put the robots back in their places.

Suddenly he spotted Zingle sitting on the floor.

"What's this mop doing here?" he gasped.

"I'm not a mop!" squeaked Zingle.

"That's not a mop," squeaked Zack quickly. "It's a very small robot."

"It doesn't look like a very small robot," said the ticket man.

"It's the latest model in the museum," said Daisy.

"I've never seen it before," replied the ticket man.

"That's because it's very small," explained Tom.

"It's a very clever robot," added Zack.

"You can ask it all sorts of questions about space," finished Tom.

"Are you sure?" asked the ticket man. He bent down to Zingle. "How many planets are there in the solar system?"

"You should know that, silly Earthling!" squeaked Zingle.

"All right then, how far away is Neptune?" asked the ticket man.

"I don't know," squeaked Zingle. "I've never been there."

"That's not a very small robot," said the ticket man. "It's just a talking mop."

"I AM NOT A MOP!" squeaked Zingle loudly. She began to roll around the floor.

"Quick!" muttered Daisy. "Do something! Zingle's getting cross."

Zack grabbed Zingle. "Its battery's getting flat," he said. "I'll switch it off."

He poked his finger into Zingle's fur.

Zingle squeaked with laughter. "That tickles!"

"Robots aren't ticklish," said the ticket man. "It must be faulty. Give it to me. I'll mend it . . ."

Ring! Ring!

The telephone was ringing once more. The ticket man hurried off to answer it.

Gronk waved his Satpad at them. "That was me again," he said proudly.

"Well done, Gronk," said Daisy. "That was close! Time to get on with our project."

In the next room there was a big rocket in the middle of the floor.

It had a sign on it.

"One day people might go into deep space in a rocket like this!" read Fizz. *"Climb aboard and enjoy the ride."*

"I want to investigate the Earth rocket," said Gronk.

They climbed in. The rocket was full of controls and switches and flashing lights.

"This will be cosmic," said Tom.

Zack pressed *start*.

There was the sound of an engine and the rocket shook. A cardboard moon wobbled past the window, followed by two stars and a lumpy-looking planet. The rocket stopped shaking.

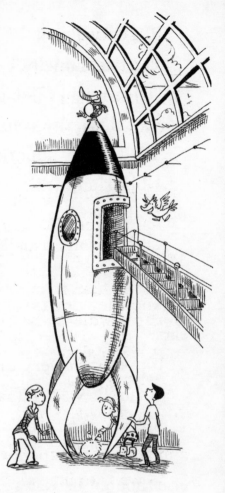

"You Earthlings aren't very good at making rockets," said Fizz.

"It didn't even fly!" squeaked Zingle.

31

"It's only a model," explained Daisy. "It can't actually fly."

"Then it looks like I've arrived just in time," said a jolly voice.

"It's Toppo!" squeaked Zingle.

A black and white stripy rabbit popped up at the window.

Rabbits don't usually have black and white stripes.

And they don't usually have corkscrew ears.

Toppo was a very unusual rabbit.

In fact he wasn't a rabbit at all.

Toppo was a Satnik. He was Tom, Zack and Daisy's class pet from school. Everyone else thought he was a zabbit – a free-range rabbit with zebra stripes.

"I decided to come and see what you were up to," said Toppo, hopping inside the rocket. "I finished investigating the school tennis racquets. Did you know that if you tie them on your feet you can ski off the staffroom roof?"

"Cosmic!" said Tom. "We'll all try that on Monday."

"Better not," said Toppo, pulling a banana skin out of his ear. "I landed in the school bins. What are you all up to?"

"We were just having a ride in this rocket," said Zack.

"But it's not a very good rocket," squeaked Zingle. "It doesn't go anywhere."

33

"My super Satpower will soon change that," declared Toppo. "Hold tight everyone and get ready for a Top Toppo Trick."

He twisted his ear.

Ping!

His Satpad flew out and landed on his paw. He tapped some keys. Then he waved it at the rocket.

The rocket rose from the ground. It flew up to the ceiling. It whooshed around the room.

"This is more like it," said Fizz.

The rocket whizzed up and down the corridor.

It zipped in and out of the robots.

It zoomed around Saturn.

Then it whooshed back and landed with a bump.

"That was amazing!" gasped Zack.

"Let's have another go," cried Tom.

"Hey!" came a shout. The ticket man burst into the room. He poked his head into the rocket. The Satniks scampered out of sight.

"What's going on?" demanded the ticket man. "I just saw this rocket whiz by."

"That's impossible," said Daisy quickly.

"This is just a model," added Zack.

"You must have seen a ghost rocket," said Tom.

The man stared at them suspiciously.

"I'll soon get rid of him," whispered Gronk from under the control panel. He tapped the keys on his Satpad.

Ring! Ring!

The ticket man didn't move.

Ring! Ring!

"The phone's ringing," said Daisy helpfully.

"It keeps doing that," said the ticket man. "But when I answer it there's no one there."

"How are we going to get rid of him?" whispered Zack.

"Emergency action," whispered Zingle from behind the captain's chair.

Whizz! Bang! Crackle!

A sparkling beam of light shot from her Satpad, flew round the ticket man and out of the door. All at once the robots marched into the room, poked their tongues out at the ticket man and marched off again.

"I won't have rude robots in my museum!" yelled the ticket man.

He chased after them.

"That'll keep him busy," squeaked Zingle.

"I've had a great idea for our school project," said Daisy. "It can be about a space flight to Saturn."

"That *is* a great idea," said Zack. "After all, we've got four Satnik experts to help us."

"But we've still got time for one more ride," Tom pointed out.

Toppo waved his Satpad at the controls. "Time for another Top Toppo Trick!" he said. "Ready for countdown?"

"Ready!" everyone yelled.

"Five," squawked Gronk.

"Four," said Daisy.

"Three," said Fizz.

"Two," said Zack.

"One," squeaked Zingle.

"LIFT OFF!" cried everyone.

The rocket shot off out of the window.

"Cosmic!" shouted Tom.

REPORT

NAME

Zingle

EARTH IDENTITY

blue mop-haired cat

REPORT

Earthling rockets are very strange. They sit in museums and don't go anywhere. No wonder Earthlings have never come to Saturn. Earthling robots are very strange. Steam comes out of their ears and their heads blow off. It's very interesting.

Best Pets

It was Saturday and Tom and Zack were on their way to school.

They didn't usually go to school on Saturdays, but today was a special day. There was going to be a pet show on the school field with lots of stalls and games.

The Satniks were going too.

Fizz was on a lead and Zingle was riding on Zack's shoulder.

They called for Daisy on the way.

Daisy waved at them from her front door.

"Where's Gronk?" asked Tom.

"I'm hiding," came Gronk's muffled voice from under Daisy's shirt.

"Who are you hiding from?" asked Fizz.

"The teachers," said Gronk solemnly. "Pets aren't supposed to go to school."

"Silly Gronk!" squeaked Zingle. "You've forgotten. Today's a special day."

"Pets are allowed at school today," Fizz reminded him.

"And we're meeting Toppo there," squeaked Zingle. "And we're all going to enter the pet show!"

Gronk poked his head out. "Are you sure?" he asked.

"Positive," said Zack.

Gronk wriggled out of Daisy's shirt, tried to take off, got his wings in a tangle and fell in a bush.

"I meant to do that," he said as Daisy pulled him out.

When they got to the school gates they saw a big sign.

"*Pet show at two o'clock,*" read Zack. "*There are events for every pet.*"

They read the list of events.

List of
Pet Show Events

1. Fastest fetching dog
2. Highest jumping rabbit
3. Loudest singing bird
4. Slitheriest snake
5. Smallest gerbil
6. Most beautiful spider
7. Pet race

"That's a very strange pet show," said Fizz. "You Earthlings have got it wrong."

"Pet show events are much better on Saturn," said Gronk.

"I'll show you," said Fizz. "I've made a list."

"Fizz is good at lists," squeaked Zingle.

Fizz twisted his ear.

Ping!

His Satpad flew out and landed on his hand.

He poked the keys with his nose.

A list wobbled in the air.

Fizz's important list about
pet show events on Saturn
by Fizz

1. Fastest fetching wibbler
2. Highest jumping satcrab
3. Loudest singing pippelpup
4. Fluffiest jinglewhopper
5. Longest smobflumber
6. And lots of others that I can't remember
7. And I mean lots
8. And a race at the end

"That's a much better list, Fizz," said Gronk. "I'll change the Earthling one. Has anyone got a pen?"

"Cosmic!" said Tom.

"It is *not* cosmic!" said Daisy.

"You can't change the list, Gronk!" said Zack.

"Why not?" asked Gronk.

"We don't have wibblers on Earth," explained Daisy.

"Or satcrabs," added Zack. "Or pippelpups."

"And we haven't got the others either," finished Daisy.

"Are you sure?" asked Fizz.

"Positive," said Daisy.

"But there'll be competitions for all of you to enter," said Tom.

"We just have to wait till two o'clock when the show starts," Zack told the Satniks.

"Plenty of time to investigate then," said Fizz, rubbing his hands together eagerly.

The school field was covered in balloons and painted signs and exciting-looking stalls. In the middle was a big arena ready for the pet show.

"This will be an excellent investigation!" squawked Gronk.

"We're off!" said Fizz.

"See you later," squeaked Zingle.

"Wait!" cried Zack. "You can't go running around on your own."

"Pets have to stay with their owners," Daisy told them.

48

"Let's go to our class stall first," said
Tom. "Toppo's meeting us there."

"What kind of stall do you think it's
going to be?" asked Zack.

"I hope it's a game," said Tom.

"It won't be *Pin the tail on the donkey*,"
laughed Daisy. "Not after the practice in
class yesterday."

"Toppo just got a bit excited," said
Zack. "He didn't mean to pin the tail onto
Miss Keane!"

"And it won't be *How many sweets in the jar*," said Zack. "Not after Toppo ate them all!"

They found their class stall. It was decorated with brightly coloured flags.

There was a sign. "It's *Guess the weight of the zabbit*," said Daisy.

"Nothing can go wrong with that," said Tom.

"Oh, yes it can!" said Zack.

Toppo was running round the stall.

Miss Keane was running after him.

Toppo waved at his friends.

"*Guess the weight of the zabbit* looks like a fun game," said Fizz.

"Can we join in?" squeaked Zingle.

"They're not playing a game," said Zack. "Miss Keane's trying to catch Toppo."

"Please get on the scales, Toppo," wailed Miss Keane. "Then I can see how much you weigh."

Toppo hid under the stall.

Miss Keane dived after him.

Toppo hopped up on top of the stall.

Miss Keane climbed up after him.

Crash!

The stall collapsed!

"I'll never find out how much Toppo

weighs," sighed Miss Keane, fighting her way out of the flags. "He won't let me catch him."

"That's because he's a free-range zabbit, Miss," Daisy reminded her. "I think you should find something else to weigh."

"We'll take Toppo with us," said Zack helpfully.

"Thanks for rescuing me," said Toppo as Tom carried him away. "Now we can all investigate the other stalls."

☆ ☆ ☆

Tom won a football
— with Fizz's help.

Zack won a
coconut — with
Toppo's help.

Daisy hooked a duck-billed parrotpuss – with Gronk's help.

"Is it time for the pet show?" squeaked Zingle.

"Not yet," said Zack. "Let's have a go on the lucky dip."

"That looks fun!" exclaimed Fizz.

Before they could stop him, he jumped into the lucky dip tub.

Soon he jumped back out, covered in sawdust and carrying a huge pile of toys.

"Are they all for us?" squeaked Zingle.

"Of course," said Fizz.

"Cosmic!" yelled Tom.

"It is *not* cosmic," said Daisy.

"You're only supposed to have one prize," explained Zack.

"We must put them back in the tub," said Daisy, "for other children to find."

"But they don't need to find them now," said Fizz, scratching his head. "I've already found them."

"It's a game," said Zack. "We'll put them back and children will have fun pulling them out."

He hid the toys in the sawdust again.

"What a strange game," said Gronk.

"Earthlings are very silly," said Toppo.

They came to a big sign. It said *Hunt the penguin*.

"*The penguin is hiding somewhere in the school field*," read Daisy. "*If you find it you can keep it*."

"I want to find the penguin!" squeaked Zingle.

"What do penguins look like?" asked Toppo.

"I know," said Gronk. "They're pink and they burrow through the earth."

"Penguins aren't pink," said Zack.

"And they don't burrow through the earth!" exclaimed Tom.

"Yes they do," said Fizz. "I'll show you."

He twisted his ear.

Ping!

His Satpad shot out and 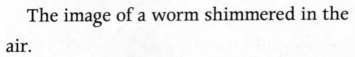 landed in his hand.

He tapped the keys.

The image of a worm shimmered in the air.

"My super Satpower will find that penguin," said Fizz.

Bleep . . . bleep . . . bleep! went his Satpad.

"That's not a penguin," said Tom. "It's a worm."

But Fizz wasn't listening. He scampered off towards a hedge.

Bleep . . . bleep . . . bleep! The bleeping got louder.

Fizz disappeared into the hedge. Earth came flying out.

BLEEP . . . BLEEP . . . BLEEP!

Fizz bounded out of the hedge, covered in mud. He had a worm on the end of his nose. "I've found the penguin!" he told the others proudly.

"Well done, Fizz!" said Gronk. "You were very quick."

"It was easy," said Fizz. "There were hundreds of them wriggling about. I'm surprised the Earthlings hadn't looked there."

"Earthlings are very silly," squeaked Zingle.

"That's not a penguin," said Zack.

"Tom told you. It's a worm."

"Are you sure?" asked Fizz.

"Positive," said Zack.

"Your Satpads are muddling up their animals as usual," explained Daisy.

"Looks like the sprungles are still flobbered," said Toppo.

"Fizz was going to mend them yesterday," squeaked Zingle.

"Zoops!" said Fizz. "I forgot. I was too busy investigating Tom's bicycle pump."

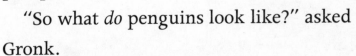

"So what *do* penguins look like?" asked Gronk.

"Penguins have black and white feathers," said Tom. "And they live where it's really cold."

"But the one you're hunting for is a toy . . ." began Daisy.

But the Satniks weren't listening.

"So penguins live where it's really cold," said Fizz thoughtfully.

"I know just where the penguin will be!" cried Gronk.

Before they could stop him, he waddled away.

Tom, Zack and Daisy set off after him through the crowd. The Satniks followed.

"There he is!" said Tom. "He's at the ice-cream cart."

Gronk was perched on the ice-cream man's head. He was poking his long tongue into the cart.

"Gronk!" yelled Daisy. "What are you doing?"

"I'm looking for the penguin," said Gronk. "He'll be right at the bottom where it's nice and cold." He pulled his tongue out of the cart. On the end was a big choc ice. Gronk swallowed it in one gulp. "There's a lot of ice cream in the way though. I'll have to eat it all."

He leant forward to get another ice cream, tripped on the man's hat and fell head first into the cart. Daisy pulled him out.

"I meant to do that," he squawked.
"And I've finished my penguin search.
He's not there."

"Your parrot's had seven lollies
already," whimpered the ice-cream man.
"And that was the
last choc ice."

"I'll pay," said
Daisy, quickly
giving him the
money.

She tucked Gronk under her arm and hurried back to the others.

"THE PET SHOW IS ABOUT TO START," came an announcement over the loudspeaker. "ALL PETS TO THE ARENA."

A man in a judge's hat was standing in the middle of the arena. He had a magnifying glass in his pocket, binoculars round his neck and he was holding a clipboard.

There was a long line of pets with their owners.

Tom, Zack and Daisy got in the queue with the Satniks.

"What on earth is that?" asked the judge, looking at Fizz.

"He's a dog," said Tom. "His name's Fizz."

"He doesn't look like a dog," said the judge.

"He's a satapoodle," said Tom. "He's a rare breed."

"Never heard of it," said the judge, writing down Fizz's name. "Who's next?"

"This is my cat, Zingle," said Zack. "She's a rare breed too."

"She looks more like a mop," said the judge.

"I'm not a mop!" squeaked Zingle.

"And she doesn't sound like a cat," said the judge.

"She's a blue mop-haired cat," said Zack

quickly. "They always miaow like that."

"Very strange," said the judge, writing down Zingle's name. "Who's next?"

"This is Gronk," said Daisy. "He's a duck-billed parrotpuss."

"I've definitely never heard of that," said the judge.

"He's very rare too," said Daisy.

The judge wrote down Gronk's name.

"I want to be in the pet show," said Toppo.

"Who said that?" asked the judge.

"Er . . . it was me," said Tom. "I want to be in the pet show."

"Don't be silly," said the judge. "You're not a pet."

Daisy picked up Toppo. "Tom means he wants *Toppo* to be in the show," she said.

"Toppo is the class zabbit."

"He looks more like a very small zebra," said the judge.

"A zabbit is a rabbit with zebra stripes," explained Zack.

"Are you sure?" said the judge suspiciously as he wrote down Toppo's name. "I don't think these are pets at all."

Tom, Zack and Daisy looked at each other in horror. Had the judge guessed that the Satniks were aliens?

"Of course they're pets," insisted Daisy. "My dad works at the Really Wild Wildlife Park so I should know."

The Satniks nodded eagerly.

The judge peered at them all through his magnifying glass.

"Very well," he said at last, "they

66

can enter the pet show. But they're the strangest pets I've ever seen."

"FIRST EVENT," came the voice from the loudspeaker. "FASTEST FETCHING DOG."

"*I'm* pretending to be a dog," said Fizz, "so I'm going to go in for that."

He ran over and joined a line of dogs. A row of helpers stood ready to throw a ball into the air for each dog. The judge stood next to them. "Ready, steady, *FETCH*!" he shouted.

The helpers threw the balls high in the air over the dogs' heads.

Fizz sat and watched them, waggling his trumpet nose.

"You have to fetch too, Fizz!" yelled Tom.

"Zoops!" said Fizz. "I forgot!"

He leapt in the air.

He caught the ball in his hand, turned three somersaults and lobbed it back to the helper.

The crowd clapped.

The judge scratched his head.

"The winner is Fizz the satapoodle," he announced at last.

Fizz waved his trumpet nose in excitement.

The judge hung a medal round Fizz's neck. "I've never seen a dog win a fetching competition that way," he said.

"Satapoodles always fetch like that," Tom told him quickly.

"NEXT EVENT," came the voice from the loudspeaker. "HIGHEST JUMPING RABBIT!"

"*I'm* pretending to be a rabbit," said Toppo, "so I'm going in for that."

Toppo lined up with four other rabbits.

"Ready, steady . . ." began the judge.

"Time for a Top Toppo Trick," whispered Toppo, waving his Satpad behind his back.

"Cosmic!" said Tom.

"It's *not* cosmic," said Zack.

"It's cheating," hissed Daisy.

"I bet there's nothing in the rules about not using super Satpowers!" said Tom.

". . . *JUMP!*" shouted the judge.

The rabbits jumped.

Toppo whooshed into the air and landed on the school roof. The crowd cheered.

The judge peered at him through his binoculars.

"The winner is Toppo the class zabbit!" he said at last.

Toppo jumped off the roof and landed on the judge's clipboard.

The judge hung a medal round Toppo's neck. "I've never seen a rabbit jump that high," he said.

"Zabbits always jump like that," said Zack.

"TIME FOR THE LOUDEST BIRD EVENT," came an announcement.

"Zoops!" said Gronk. "*I'm* pretending to be a parrot and parrots are very loud birds, so I'm going to go in for that."

A mynah bird, a cockatoo and a budgerigar were sitting on a perch.

Gronk flapped up to join them. He got his wings in a tangle, crash-landed on the end of the perch and catapulted the other birds into the air.

"I meant to do that!" he squawked.

"Ready, steady . . . *SING*!" called the judge.

The birds all began singing at once.

The mynah bird chirped *Five Little Ducks*.

The cockatoo squawked *Happy Birthday*.

The budgerigar warbled *Polly Put the Kettle On*.

"Time for the song of the crested natnurbler," announced Gronk, twiddling his whiskers.

Ping!

His Satpad flew out of his feathers. He hid it under his wing and tapped the keys with his bill.

"Oh, no," said Daisy. "He's going to use his super Satpower."

A terrible noise filled the air.

It sounded like squealing tyres and breaking glass mixed together.

The crowd put their fingers in their ears.

The birds' feathers stood on end.

All the dogs in the pet show began to howl.

"Stop!" shouted the judge.

Gronk turned off his Satpad.

"How did he make that noise?" the judge asked Daisy.

"Duck-billed parrotpusses always sing like that," said Daisy.

"Shall I do it again?" asked Gronk hopefully.

"No!" screeched the crowd.

"The winner of the loudest bird competition," said the judge quickly, "is Gronk the duck-billed parrotpuss."

He threw a medal round Gronk's neck and went off to judge the next competition.

"TIME FOR THE SLITHERIEST SNAKE EVENT," came another announcement.

"Can I go in for that?" squeaked Zingle.

"No," said Zack.

"Why not?" squeaked Zingle.

"Because you're not slithery enough," said Zack.

"Then I'll enter the smallest gerbil event," squeaked Zingle.

"You're not small enough," said Daisy.

"What about the most beautiful spider event?" squeaked Zingle.

"You haven't got enough legs," said Tom.

"I don't like this pet show after all," squeaked Zingle.

"You can go in for the race at the end," said Daisy.

"Zoops!" squeaked Zingle crossly. "I can't wait that long. I'm off."

"Where are you going?" asked Tom.

"I'm going to hunt the penguin instead," squeaked Zingle.

"Don't forget it's got black and white feathers," Toppo reminded her.

"And it lives where it's very cold," added Fizz.

"Not this one," said Daisy. "I tried to tell you. The penguin you're looking for is a toy . . ."

But the Satniks weren't listening.

Zingle scampered away.

"After her," cried Zack.

Zingle ran up to the hot-dog stand.

"Not cold enough for the penguin here," she squeaked.

She whizzed through the tea tent.

"Too hot in there," she squeaked.

She came to the *Soak the caretaker* stall. Mr Broom the caretaker was poking his head through a wooden wall. In front of the wall was a bucket of water. Next to the bucket was a sponge.

Zingle peered into the bucket. "This is nice and cold," she squeaked. "Are you in there, penguin?"

But just then a little boy bent down and picked her up.

"He thinks she's a sponge!" said Tom.

"Zingle hates getting wet!" groaned Zack.

"Stop!" yelled Daisy.

But it was too late.

The little boy dunked Zingle in the water and threw her at the caretaker.

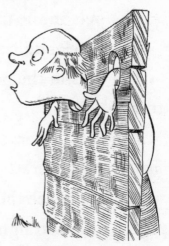

SPLAT!

Zingle bounced off the caretaker's nose, landed on the grass and began to roll about, squeaking crossly.

"TIME FOR THE PET RACE," said the announcer.

"Zingle's going to miss the race!" wailed Daisy.

All the pets lined up at the starting line, but Zingle was rolling around the school field.

"Come back, Zingle!" called Zack.

"Ready, steady, *GO!*" called the judge.

The pets in the pet race set off.

Tom, Zack and Daisy chased after Zingle.

The pets in the pet race raced along the track.

Zingle rolled around the field, faster and faster.

She didn't see the starting line.

She rolled straight over it.

She caught up with the pets in the pet race.

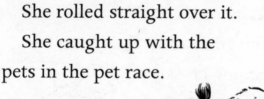

She rolled past the pot-bellied pig who was in third place.

She rolled past the donkey who was in second place.

She rolled past the greyhound who was sprinting away in the lead.

Zingle didn't see the finishing line.

She rolled straight over it.

The crowd cheered.

"Stop, Zingle!" called Daisy. "You've won the race!"

But Zingle didn't stop rolling.

Tom, Zack and Daisy ran after her. Fizz, Toppo and Gronk chased after them.

Zingle crashed into a flowerbed and disappeared in a shower of petals.

She came out again, dragging something huge. It was black and white and fluffy.

"What's that?" asked Toppo.

"I don't know," squeaked Zingle. "It was hiding in there. It was too scared to move so I've helped it out."

"You've found the penguin!" cried Zack.

"Silly Earthling," squeaked Zingle. "This isn't a penguin."

"It hasn't got any feathers," said Gronk.

"And it's not cold in that flowerbed," said Toppo.

"It's a *toy* penguin," explained Daisy.

"Zoops!" squeaked Zingle. "Why didn't you say so?"

"A *toy* penguin!" exclaimed Fizz. "I know just what we have to do with toys."

He took the penguin by the beak and began to drag it back towards the flowerbed.

"Where are you going?" asked Tom.

"It's a toy penguin," said Fizz, "so it has to go back where it came from, just like the lucky dip toys."

"You don't have to do that," said Tom. "Zingle found it so you can keep it!"

"Are you sure?" asked Gronk.

"Positive!" said Tom.

"But where will it live?" asked Daisy. "It's a bit big."

"Zack's gran would love it," squeaked Zingle. "It could sit on her lap."

"I'm not sure . . ." said Zack.

"I'll look after it," said Gronk. "I could teach it to fly!"

"That would be great!" said Tom.

"No, it wouldn't," said Daisy.

"We could give it to Miss Keane,"
suggested Toppo. "It would cheer her up."

"*That* is a great idea," said Daisy.

"We'd better get Zingle dry now,"
Zack told the others, "before she gets
cross again."

Pin the tail on the
donkey
How many sweets
in the jar?
Guess the weight
of the zabbit teacher
Guess the name
of the
PENGUIN

FUN FUN FOR
FUN EVERYONE

"But I'm not wet," squeaked Zingle.

"You're right," said Tom, patting Zingle's head. "You must have rolled so fast you dried yourself."

"Of course I did, silly Earthling!" squeaked Zingle. "I love pet shows. Now, when's my race?"

"You've just won it!" Daisy told her.

"Are you sure?" squeaked Zingle.

"Positive!" said Daisy.

"Then where's my medal?" squeaked Zingle.

"COULD THE WINNER OF THE PET RACE PLEASE COLLECT THEIR MEDAL?" said the announcer.

"That's me!" squeaked Zingle.

She ran up to the judge.

The judge got out his magnifying glass.

"Are you sure this isn't a mop?" he asked suspiciously.

"Positive," said Zack.

"I'm not a mop," squeaked Zingle.

The judge glared at Zingle.

"Blue mop-haired cats always miaow like that," Daisy reminded him.

The judge hung a medal around Zingle. He looked at the Satniks.

"You have got the most amazing pets I have ever seen," said the judge.

"You're right," said Daisy.

"They're out of this world!" said Zack.

"They're cosmic!" said Tom.

REPORT

NAME

Fizz

EARTH IDENTITY

satapoodle

REPORT

Earth penguins are strange. They have feathers and live in cold places. Toy Earth penguins have fur and live in flowerbeds.

Earthling games are strange. If you find toys in a tub, you have to put them all back again.

But if you find a penguin in a flowerbed, you can keep it.